T0064110

TAT

TAT

The Adam's Tale

Ravi Teja

PARTRIDGE

A Penguin Random House Company

Copyright © 2015 by Ravi Teja.

ISBN:	Hardcover	978-1-4828-4623-2
	Softcover	978-1-4828-4622-5
	eBook	978-1-4828-4621-8

Print information available on the last page.

To order additional copies of this book, contact
Partridge India
000 800 10062 62
orders.india@partridgepublishing.com

www.partridgepublishing.com/india

*Dedicated to the
three most important people
in my life*

- ➢ *MOM*

- ➢ *DAD*

- ➢ *FRIENDS*

ACKNOWLEDGEMENTS

The biggest thing which I was dreaming about is to become an author. To achieve it the foremost thing which a debut writer needed is encouragement. There are many hands who helped me to produce this book.

Firstly, my parents Ashok Kumar and Rama Devi including my sweet sister Harshitha had done the best which they could do to help me in completing this book.

My friends Srilekha, Abhilash, Likitha, Madhuri, Srinivas, Zubair, Chetan, Rahul, Manisha Sen Gupta, Abhishek, Aishwarya and Swathi had stayed right with me till the end in the process and gave an honest review for my book. I feel like it's a god gift to have such a lovely friends.

There are even behind the script scenes where four guys Arun, Ravindranath Tagore, Sumanth and Kalyan used to make nasty jokes about my script to cheer me up. It's a funny thing that I have included some of them.

A special thanks is required for my guru Mrs. Padmavathi. She provided me with required tips to complete this book.

My Trustworthy Editor Rakesh Kumar had produced my manuscript in a professional way.

The cover design by my friends Sunay Dawson and Hari Krishna is one of the best parts of my book.

Last, but not the least a heart full thanks to my publishing consultant Marveric Pana and to the Partridge India Publications for being such an interactive and to produce this book.

CONTENTS

CHAPTER-1

MISSION TO EARN BUCKS

The time was around 8 a. m, my phone began to ring. The call was from Mr.William.

"Hello! Adam pick up at Edson square. You got 15 minutes left to reach that place", he said and ended the call.

He used to keep such filthy restrictions to earn more customers. If we exceed that time limit for every extra one minute we need to pay in return $5, which he used to cut from our wages.

I had to hurry up to save my money. Usually, I used to keep my taxi in my Uncle's garage, as I don't have sufficient space to fit my car in my garage, which was filled up with junk and garbage. I don't even find time to clean it, as Mr.William would always give me a call whenever I felt to clean it. I rushed to my Uncle's garage.

"Uncle Patrick, I need my taxi as fast as I can", I screamed.

He immediately threw the keys of that garage as he understood my position of urgency. I have only 10 minutes left. One thing was badly running in my mind "If the customer takes off my money then surely I have to wait for one more month to party, as I already lost halt of it".

I shouted "Bye Uncle! Catch you in the evening", and started the car.

Eight more minutes left, even though Mr.William keeps these restrictions he generally gives us the destiny of our nearest places to reach. So, eight minutes are enough for me to drive up to the Edson square.

There you go found my business minded customer wearing a brown colored jacket and ignoring me as the time would run off. I came to know about him as Mr.William also had another business tactics of saving every old customer photo with his name and sending them back to us.

I called him "Excuse me, Sir! UFO cabs hired for you".

"Yeah, take me to the Techanalysis in Manhattan," the man said.

"Sure, sir! At your service," I said and started my taxi.

I have a habit of speaking to the customers whoever boards my taxi until they reach their destination. Some of them feel comfortable with it, while others used to just node their head and barely listen to me. The person who just boarded my car began to read the newspaper and opened the stock exchange column.

"Your good name, Sir?" I asked him.

"My name is Marshall", he said.

As, I cannot stop myself talking towards him after asking his name, I started giving work to my mouth.

"Where do you work, Sir?" I asked him.

"I work as a marketing supervisor at the Techanalysis and there's an important meeting for me to attend at 9a.m.", he replied me.

This man seemed to be a little brilliant; he even answered my next question without giving strain to my mouth.

I asked, "I just want to invest some of my amount in those stock markets. Will you give me a perfect analysis on which to invest?"

The man gave a strange look towards me and with a healthy smile he said, "See young man, if I give an advice to invest on so and so company and what if by chance that company gets huge loses. You are going to lose whole of your money. Better keep an eye on only one source by choosing the best".

I thought for a while that he was right as I had chosen the worst source as a taxi driver. Need to find a better one!!

I shut my mouth for few minutes after such a good lecture.

Suddenly, Marshall asked, "Do you think that the source you have chosen is right for you income?"

I was shocked and looked at him. Whether he had read my mind? No chance, but he was very opt to my thinking. May be a mere guess? Hope so.

"No sir, but I need to find much better one than this", I replied him.

He gave a wild smile and said, "Think about it, man. You'll find it". We reached the destination.

"Sir, can you suggest me a job which can fit with my appearance?" I asked Marshall.

"You have a fair height of about 5 feet 10 inches I guess. A little muscled body and your outfits don't represent you as a taxi driver. Think of starting your career as an Entrepreneur. It may fit for you. You do also have an attractive face", Marshall replied.

Those words really made me think that I'm cool enough!!

"Thank you for your suggestion sir", I said.

He gave me the money and raised his hat, as to take me it as a symbol to say, "Bye". I waved the hand in air and started the taxi. Until, Mr.William sends me another image of customer I can run my taxi for nearby destinations. You might be thinking "What if he sends an image to pick up someone when you are in the middle of dropping a customer?" It's very simple according to Mr.William, just drop him off and reach the place which I say within the time. Screw his bloody rules!! . But I had no option he was the one and only person who pay good wages.

I need to look for one more fare. After, speaking to such a civilized person my mind began to think "Not one more of that kind for today." My phone began to ring; it was another call from Mr.William.

"Hello! Adam, a rich customer to pick up this time. Pick him up at Trinity church by 12:00p.m", he said.

"Sure, sir!" I said. That was the only thing I could say.

He indirectly mentioned me that you got one hour free time since the time was 11:00a.m. So, pick up at least one more customer and gain some money. There was no option left for me, I had to say yes.

"Taxi!!"I heard it at a distance and rotated my head 45 degrees towards right. There she is a lady of age between 30 to 35 years.

I said, "UFO cabs! Where can I take you madam?"

"Take me to the 9th Avenue Nolita ", she replied.

It could take me barely 20 minutes to reach that place. So, I started my taxi and my mouth began to work.

"Looks like a fine morning to start the shopping ", I said.

She gave me a smirk and enquired "Yes, it is .Are you feeling to do it?"

"I was speaking about you," I replied.

"Oh, I'm sorry. Actually, I am moving there to meet a person not for shopping", she replied.

"I felt you were about to buy something by your moves", I replied.

She gave a tiniest smile which remained a fraction of second on her face and asked, "That's ok. Can I guess something from your moves?"

It seemed a little interesting about what she might guess from my moves.

So, undoubtedly I replied, "Yeah! Sure, move on".

"You are a little tensed about something, aren't you?" She asked.

"The only nervousness I feel now is to drop you as fast as I can so as to save my wages from donating it to my customers", I was about to speak these lines to her but we reached the Nolita. She opened the door and started moving towards a person who was standing in front of my taxi. He moved towards me.

"What?" I yelled.

He gave me the money and left the place with her. Immediately, I started my taxi and started driving to Trinity church, where I need to pick up that one big customer mentioned by my boss. Finally, I reached that place and it was about 11:50a.m. I took a breath for few seconds and started looking around to find him.

Suddenly, I felt someone tapped my shoulder. I gave a 180 degree rotation for my face to see, he was that one big customer.

I started to speak my polite speech "UFO cabs!! Where can I take you sir?"

He opened his bag and gave me an envelope. Then he started dialing someone from his phone and gave it to me.

I asked the person in the phone, "Hello! Who is it?"

"Adam! It's me, William. Do whatever that man says and he should be satisfied by your service. Finish the work immediately", he said and ended the call.

My boss even started to use me as a servant other than a taxi driver.

The big customer started to speak "Take this envelope to 5th avenue central park, a man with a black shirt and cream colored trouser will be waiting and it should be reached before 3p.m. A very important thing about it is don't even try to open it. If I figure it out that you tried it, the consequences will be very painful".

What would I do with that bloody envelope? I just nodded my head and took the envelope. I need my wages and that was the only thing which I could do to get them. The place was a little far for me to drive, but to my goodness I drove up to that place within 2 hours and dispatched that envelope to the person mentioned by the customer. I returned to my Uncle's garage after that forceful work and parked my taxi inside the garage.

CHAPTER-2

"SHE" ENTERS MY LIFE

Every day, I used Mr.William phone call as an alarm. Surprisingly, the time which he used to call me was between 8a.m to 9a.m every day and at most in my entire taxi carrier it was 9:30a.m.My phone began to ring.

"Hello! Adam pick up at space market and you got only 30 minutes to reach it", said Mr.William.

"Got it", I said and ended the call.

It takes me hardly 20 min to drive to that place. So, no more hurry is required for me. I need to move towards the garage now.

Uncle Patrick was watering the plants.

"Good morning, Adam. Pleasant day", he said noticing me at a distance.

"Good morning, Uncle. Indeed a pleasant day. Can I have the garage keys?" I asked him.

"Sure, young man. They are in the cupboard, go get them", he replied.

I entered his house which was a spacious one. I moved upstairs as the cupboard is in his bedroom. There was a huge photo frame of uncle with a man who was about the age of the uncle.

After moving towards the garage, I asked uncle "who was the man in that photo near the cupboard?"

"He is Dr.Robert a well-known friend of mine. He is a very famous doctor, who works at Lenox hospital," uncle replied.

"His face and body posture seemed to me like a doctor", I said "so, my guess was right".

"Bye, Uncle. See you in the evening", I said and started the taxi.

Within 15 minutes I reached the place. But it began to rain heavily, after such sweet words of uncle "pleasant day". A man knocked my door, I opened my window luckily he was the person whom Mr.William said me to pick up. But, something different happened here. A girl came running towards my taxi, opened the door and sat inside.

The man said "Drop her at 1230 York Avenue, Rockfeller University".

He left the place. She started to rub her curly hair after having exposed to the rain. My eyes were staring at her.

"Start the taxi man. Why are you starting at me?" she questioned which made me smile.

I started the taxi. She has sharp and beautiful eyes, which looked as the most attractive part on her face. Usually,

I don't shut my mouth while driving. After seeing such a charming face, how can I stop myself from talking to her?

But, this time I felt a little hesitation to speak with my customer. I don't know why? But, I managed to overcome it. Her expressions looked like she was tensed about something.

"Looks like you are a bit tensed about something", I said her finally.

"Yes, I need to give a presentation today. So, at least a little tension is required for me to perform well", she replied looking through the window.

She suddenly opened her MAC and got involved in it. I started to think of dragging her mind from it.

"So, are you a science student?" I asked her.

"I am a zoologist, at a beginner stage", she answered me.

"Zoologist! That sounds good. I love birds, especially parrots", I said.

"What!!! I study animals not birds. The one who studies birds are called ornithologists", she said which made me feel like "Don't even speak about those things which you are not aware off".

"You said zoologist. That sounded me like ornithologists", I tried to cover my sentence.

But she didn't even reply me instead. I tried it again.

"Do you study about a specific animal?" I asked.

"No, but I am trying to keep my attention on chameleons. I have a keen interest towards them from my child hood. So, I choose them", she replied.

"Chameleon, a different kind of animal indeed", I said.

Without making any eye contact with me she said, "I do love the strange ones".

A one line answer with a bitter tone that was enough for me to understand that she was involved in her MAC and not to disturb her. But, I couldn't keep myself without speaking to my passengers.

So, I asked "Do you think that the color changing capability of chameleons is supernatural?"

This time I got a reaction from her, a strange look at my face saying "What!! Are you kidding? You are speaking to a science student and you speak about super natural things".

I laughed to support up my statement and said, "I was implying that, then what's the reason behind it?"

There was no answer from her for few seconds. I thought she might be involved again in the presentation stuff. But, to my surprise she started speaking.

"It has got some mechanism to change its color. I cannot explain it for you right now, as I have to deal with my presentation".

After such a nasty reply from her, I could do nothing but minding my own business. We remained silent for few minutes. Suddenly, she opened her phone and her face expressions changed to a terror side.

A sweet voice came from her side "Excuse me! Can I please lend your phone to make a call? My battery is dead".

What could you think my answer will be? "Sure, why not?" I said and gave my mobile. Obviously that was the one I would say. She gave a cutest smile and took my phone. She started dialing the numbers and moved her curly hair to the back of her ear.

"Hello! I am Lisa. Is it started?"

"Thank god! Lucky day for me".

"Yeah, I'll be there within 10 minutes".

"Bye", she spoke and gave back my phone. We remained silent for few seconds.

"My name is Lisa and you?" she asked me.

To my amazement she closed her MAC and finally spoke to me.

"Adam" I replied.

I took it as a symbol for asking me to speak with her.

"How many years it would take for you to understand it completely?" I asked her.

She sighed and said "A lifetime".

"Oh, my god! A lifetime. So you are going to spend a lifetime on your strange creature", I asked.

"I just want to study it and find at least one new unrevealed characteristics of that animal. It would really be a satisfactory one for me", she replied with a pleasant answer.

That was indeed a perfect answer what we can expect from a science student. Finally, we reached the university. She paid me the money and started to move as fast as she can without looking back at me. I just opened my car door and felt as if she is in the car.

Then I got two more pickups from Mr.William which I drove off in no time and started to drive back towards the garage.

Uncle Patrick was waiting outside his house for someone. He gave a smile by watching me through a distance. I parked my taxi and moved towards the uncle and asked "what's the matter? Are you waiting for someone?"

"I was waiting for you my son", uncle replied.

"Oh! Is there a problem with me?" I enquired.

"Not at all. I need to ask you for some help", uncle replied.

"Really!! What is it about?" I asked.

"You need to get my reports and medicines from my friend whom you asked about in the morning", uncle replied.

Uncle Patrick doesn't ask me for any help. If he asks then I would do it for sure because he is a very kind hearted and a well-known person to me.

So, I said "Yes, uncle. Don't worry I will get them tomorrow".

He gave the address of that place and offered me a cup of tea. I drank it and left the place to my house, hoping not to receive any more calls from Mr.William until tomorrow morning. And I need to speak with him in the morning, as I need to ask him to grant me 3 hours to get those reports. Hopefully, Mr.William knows my uncle and he will grant me the next minute I ask him about it.

CHAPTER-3

A FANCY OFFER

I spoke to Mr.William about my Uncle's work; he undoubtedly gave me permission to move on. I started moving towards the garage. Uncle was waiting outside his house for me to arrive.

"Good morning, uncle. Your work will be done", I said.

Uncle gave a smile and said "That is why I chose you to get them".

Then I started my taxi saying "Bye!" to uncle.

He gave me the address of the hospital where I can find that doctor.

"Lenox hospital
100 East 77th street
New York."

The hospital was a little far from the place I live. Now, I don't even have a passenger to speak with. So, I thought of thinking about something. The first thought that struck me was about the Lisa. "Has she completed her presentation successfully? It was an easy task for her or ...." These things began to run in my mind. I couldn't concentrate on my driving and suddenly a truck came facing towards me. I turned the car to my right and applied breaks.

Thank god! Saved myself from a fatal accident. I took breathe for a while and started driving to the hospital. This time I cleaned up my mind and focused on my driving. I reached the hospital and moved to the reception.

"I need to meet Dr.Robert", I said.

"Do you have an appointment?" she enquired me.

"No but, tell him Mr. Patrick sent me here to meet him", I responded.

She called to the doctor and said to me, "You can meet him in the second floor and the room number is 204, sir".

That was indeed a much big hospital and I started to move towards his room. I used the lift to reach his cabin and I entered into it.

"Are you the one Patrick sent to meet me?" doctor asked.

"Yes, my name is Adam. Uncle Patrick wants some reports and medicines from you", I replied.

"Sure, here you go", he said and gave them to me.

"What sort of work do you do?" he enquired me.

"I am a taxi driver", I replied.

"A Taxi driver! Do you get enough salary to meet your basic needs?" he questioned me.

"No sir. I do adjust myself to overcome those problems", I replied.

"It's a pity thing. Can I help you out from it?" the doctor asked.

He might be expecting something from me so I asked, "What can I do for you?"

"Oh! Did you get my point? It's not a big task. I test my drugs on animals and humans. At most every drug I produced was successful. So, I need your body to test it", doctor said.

He wants to test them on me. Oh my god! I was so scared. I stood up and started to leave the room.

Doctor said, "Wait man!! Think for a while, you can get more money. All your problems will be solved".

He walked towards me and gave me his card. I took it and kept it immediately in my pocket, without having a look at it. What if he tests a wrong drug on me? I cannot let it happen for the sake of money. I moved out from the hospital and drove back to the uncle's house.

The door was closed, I rang the bell. A voice came "The door is open, get in". I entered the house and uncle was in his room. He took the medicines and reports from me. My mind was filled up with that drugs stuff. So, I just calmly left uncle's house and moved towards my house.

The doctor already said that most of his drugs worked well then, why to fear? I can get some money and look for some other job other than this taxi work.

Oh, god!! I couldn't understand my situation to say yes or no. This is like a do or die situation for me. To do it or to die as a taxi driver. He said he can give me more money and I can eliminate Mr.William from my life. If the drug fails and I die? Oh no! I cannot let this happen. I was unable to keep my mind stable on one thing. God, please show me way out of this puzzle.

CHAPTER-4

BLIND BELIEF-I

Suddenly, I woke up to the sound of my phone ring. I found myself lied down on the table. I just gave a look at the clock it was 9a.m. So, the call might be from my dear boss.

"Hello! Adam, what's the matter? This is the 10th time I am calling you today. Are you drunk?" he started questioning as if I was going to sell his whole taxi stand.

"No, sir. I'm not drunk, but I need a leave today. I am not at all feeling well. Please spare me this day", I requested him.

"It's ok. I'll hire some other person. But, you need to work an extra day for me. I won't leave you", he said and ended the call.

Oh, not again. An extra day, this is not at all fare. Why can't I just have a leave for one day? Screw his business mind. I don't want to work with him. Drug or whatever it is I will join hands with that doctor. At least, he is a little softer than this incensed boss. I started to check my pockets for the visiting card of that Doctor.

"Yeah!! I found it", I yelled. I dialed his number and spoke, "Hello! Doctor Robert. It's Adam and I am ready to test the drug on me".

Doctor laughed and said, "I know no one's going to refuse my offer. Meet me at my laboratory which is at R laboratory

220 West

85th street

New York".

First of all I need to speak about how much money he is going to give me for it. If he refuses to give more money, I won't leave him until I get them. I don't want to lead my life anymore as a taxi driver.

Why did he ask me to come for the laboratory, other than hospital? He might start testing on me from today itself. In that case, I can get my money today itself. All these thoughts began to run in my mind. I started to drive to the lab, hoping for the best. This is like a judgment day for me. If the drug succeeds, I can live my life happily. If I fail, I can say goodbye to my world.

Even, I didn't say to my uncle about this because he won't let me do this and it might create a dispute between them.

I reached the lab within no time thinking about all these things. The lab was situated a little outside the city. There was even much security for it.

"Oh, Jesus! Save me", I said and moved in. A man came towards me and asked "Are you Mr. Adam?"

I nodded my head and he started to take me to the doctor's room. The room was a spacious one with all the equipment's in it. I don't even know what they are.

Doctor came towards me and asked "Are you ready for it?"

"Yes, I am. First of all I need to know how much you are going to pay for it", I enquired.

Doctor laughed and said "$10000. Is it enough?"

I just thought for a while that my life is settled and said "I didn't expect that you are going to give me $10000. My imagination stopped around $5000 to $6000".

He gave me a paper and asked to sign it.

"What is this for?" I questioned him.

"Just an agreement that we are not responsible if you die in the middle of the process", he answered me.

I came prepared for it. So, I signed and gave it to him. He asked me to remove dress and to lie down on that bed. I felt a little terrified and lied down on it. He asked me to keep my mind free of thoughts.

The doctor's don't even know what to speak. Can anyone keep thoughts off his mind in a situation like this? But, I don't have a choice I need to do what he says otherwise it's a danger for me.

He asked me to close my eyes and said that he is going to drug me to make me sleep first. He injected it and I felt everything was normal for some time. The doctors started to work with their equipment's on my body. My eyes began to close and I feel asleep within no time.

CHAPTER-5

INCIDENT THAT RUINED ME

Slowly, I got consciousness and opened my eyes one of that doctor's shouted, "He is conscious now".

I just raised my hand to get up. I was stunned to see what just happened to me. My skin had been transplanted. I was not able to feel it. It suddenly changed its color to silver. My heartbeat began to rise. The skin became red in color now and again slowly to silver. Oh, my god! What had these doctors done to me?

I started screaming loudly, "You bastards what have you done?"

All the doctors ran towards me. I couldn't control my anger. I started to beat them.

I grabbed Doctor Roberts collar and shouted, "You scoundrel I believed you, but you have cheated me. I accepted to test the drug on me but you done something else for me".

"Listen…………Listen………." Doctor said in a moaning voice.

I punched on his face and threw him aside. Four doctors came running towards me and grabbed my two hands. A doctor gave me anesthesia from my back.

I shouted loudly, "Oh, God!!" and pushed those doctors.

My eyes began to close slowly. "I'm … going to….. Kill…. You….." I said and lost consciousness.

After sometime, I got my sense again. If I shout again then these doctors are going to inject me again. So, I remained calm and looked around me with half eyes opened. Still, the doctors are working on something. I had to wait for some time to make my moves. If anyone of those doctors found me awake, then they are going to implement their next plan on me. So, I need to be careful to get out of here. I began to recall the path which I entered the laboratory.

First, I have seen two security guards outside, then I moved into a lawn where a person came and took me to the Robert's room. Presently, I am in his room. So, I need a plan to move from here.

Starting point is to get out of this room. The people here are doctors not wrestlers, so I can easily beat them. But, there's a problem here, they have a powerful weapon "Anesthesia". The last two times, it was drugged to me by the same person. So, I need to knock him down first. I need a right time to do it. So, I waited for the whole night.

The time was around 3a.m, all the doctors left the room except the one who drugged me. This is the right time for me to move on. I spotted the position of the doctor in the room and the syringe was also placed beside his chair. I took a deep breath and ran towards the doctor. He raised his mouth to shout; I grabbed his neck and closed his mouth with my hand. I took the syringe and injected it to him. One down and many to go.

But, I don't have any idea of the situation outside the room. I gave work to my brain. The next moment an idea struck to my mind.

I removed the doctor's dress and began to wear it. I was frightened to see my skin and moved towards the mirror. These bastards have ruined me; I am not a human anymore. My skin began to change its color again to dark red.

I wore the doctor's dress and covered my entire body with gloves, scarf's etc. so that no one can find me. The door was not locked. I opened it and began to walk. The lawn was empty, but two security guards are guarding the lab from outside. I need to manage them to get out of here. So, I checked around whether there is any other exit. There was no other exit but, I found an alarm on the wall adjacent to the entrance of the laboratory. If I press it, then these guards will run towards the doctor's room thinking that I am in there. So, I can escape easily by doing it.

I started moving according to the plan and rang the alarm. But only one of them ran towards the room, the other one was still guarding the entrance.

I moved towards him and said "The other guard needs your help".

He gave a look at my ID card which I stole from my drug partner, while wearing his dress and ran towards the room. That's it!!! I am out of the lab and took my taxi to drive back to my room.

CHAPTER-6

AN UNEXPECTED THOUGHT

I drove as fast as I can to reach my room and checked my rear window whether anyone is following me. Thank god!! I overtook them and reached my room.

If I park my car in my uncle's garage, then surely he will ask me, why did I wear doctor's suit? I cannot explain the whole thing to him, he will be frightened.

So, I parked the taxi outside my house and moved in. Oh, god! What should I do now? To whom should I consult? If this news gets out, then everyone is going to look me like an alien. I gave a look towards my skin again and thought "Okay! I am able to change the color of my skin. What am I?" "A chameleon". This is not at all god. I need to get out of this. Think Adam. Someone spoke to me about chameleons earlier. Who is it?

Lisa was the one who spoke to me about this she said that she was going to give a presentation on these chameleons. I need to contact her immediately. But, how can I? I don't even know her mobile number. She used my mobile on that day to contact someone. So, I checked my dialed calls on that day.

Thank god!! I found it. I called to that number. The user was busy. I tried it again. This time the user responded.

"Hello! Can I speak to Lisa?" I asked.

"This is Mary and I am Lisa's friend", she replied.

"Listen! Listen! Please for god sake get me Lisa on the call. This is very urgent, I need to talk to her immediately", I said.

"Ok. I'll pass the phone", she said and gave the phone to Lisa.

"Hello! This is Lisa. Who is it?" she asked me.

That sounded really good.

"It's me Adam. I just dropped you at your college on that day while you were preparing for your presentation", I said.

"Oh!! Got you. What's the matter?" she asked.

"I need to meet you as soon as possible. There's something I cannot tell you on the phone call. You are the right person who can solve my problem. Please, do believe me. It's a matter of life and death for me", I said to her with a low tone. She gave a silence for a while.

"Okay! Where should I meet you?" she asked.

"40th street
410 west
New York", I said.

"I will be there within half an hour", she said and ended the call.

I heard the sound of someone knocking my door. I slowly, moved towards it and opened the door. It was an expected guest. "Lisa".

"What happened to you?" she asked me.

"Please, get in", I said.

"Why did you cover your entire body?" she questioned.

"There's something I should show you please don't scream", I whispered and showed my skin to her.

She gave a loud scream and ran towards the entrance. I covered my skin and stopped her.

"Listen to me. A doctor had cheated me. He told me that he was going to test a drug on me. But, he did something else on me. So here I am in search of you. Please, don't get frighten and run away from me. You are my last hope. Show me a way out of this situation", I said to convince her.

She sat on the chair and gave a look towards me.

"Ok, I understand your position. But, I need to talk to my professor about this. He can help you to find a solution for it", she said with a saddest stone.

I need to meet another person now. She went to the corner of my room and started to speak with her professor.

"We need to go to his house. He will be able to test your skin there", she said.

"Do I have any option other than that?" I spoke to myself and said "Oh, yes. Let's move" and started to drive to his house. I felt a little happy this time because Lisa was with me again in my car. But, I remained silent until I drove to his house.

CHAPTER-7

WHAT'S MY SITUATION

We reached the professor's house and Lisa knocked his door. A man came and opened the door.

"Good evening, sir", Lisa said.

"Oh, yeah. Good evening, get in", a voice came from that man.

"Is he your professor?" I asked Lisa.

"Yes. His name is Phil burg", she replied me.

We moved into the house. He took us straight away to his lab. But, this was a little one when compared with the laboratory which gave me this.

The professor took a sample of my blood and also peeled out a part of my skin. He started to examine it and wrote something about it. Lisa was also in a nail-biting situation of what's going to happen? Just like me.

Doctor came towards me and said, "Listen to me carefully. That doctor had transplanted a chameleon skin to you. I don't know how he had done it. But, these chameleons do contain specialized cells named chromatophores in them. These are a bit responsible for the color change. But, when I compared these chromatophores content between you and the chameleons, I found a thing very interesting".

"The chromatophores content in you is thrice the number which a normal chameleon has", Phil burg said.

I don't even know whether it is good news or a bad news.

I just asked him "so, how can I change my skin's color?"

"When you touch an object the light reflects from it passes on to your skin. The chromatophores present in your upper most skin layer which is xanthophores are going to detect and passes that information to your deepest skin layer which contains the melanin pigment, it is responsible for the change of your skin color. So, the color is going to be equally distributed on your skin", professor said.

I just removed mask on my face and touched the chair which was in the dark brown color. Slowly, my skin color matched it. Now, I am able to feel it. Professor and Lisa were staring at me.

"So, this is it?" I asked him.

"I just gave a brief thing to make you understand", the professor said with a smile.

"How can I become a normal human?" I questioned him.

"You need to meet that doctor again. He might have an answer for it because he was the one who designed it for you", the professor replied.

I am not only going to meet him but also going to kill him.

"Thank you, professor. You made me to understand my state", I said to him.

He gave me a smile and said "Hope to see you again as a human".

I just dropped Lisa at her home and started to drive back to my room. Now, I need to find a way to meet that doctor. But, how can I meet him? I just know two of his places. One is his hospital and the other one is his laboratory. If I move to the laboratory, than surely those security guards are going to catch me and take me to the same room from where I escaped. And the hospital wasn't an easy place to find him. It is full of security and people working in there. I lied down on bed thinking of what to do.

CHAPTER-8

BLIND BELIEF-II

The sunrays fell on my eyes directly from the window and I woke up. I felt everything was normal for few minutes until, I saw my skin.

My phone began to ring. It was none other than Mr.William. I didn't attend the call and put my phone in silent mode. I need to meet that doctor now.

After thinking for few minutes, I got a point that the doctor was my uncle's friend. And he might know his address. So, it would be safe for me to call him rather than meeting him.

So, I called and asked, "Uncle Patrick, this is Adam. Can I have the address of that doctor in your photo?"

"Oh, yes. I can give it to you. But why do you need it all of a sudden?" uncle enquired me.

"I have a health problem and need to meet him personally to speak about it", I replied.

Uncle gave me the address of that doctor's house.

"Take care, uncle. I will meet you in the evening", I said.

It became a habit to me to say him that I will be meeting him in the evening as I used to park my taxi in his garage and speak with him for a while.

Doctor Robert, here I come.

I started to drive to his house and called Lisa to say that I was going to the doctor's house and if you don't receive a call from me within two to three days. Please inform the cops about it.

I parked my car at the corner of that street and began to walk towards his house. I straight away walked up to his entrance and rang the bell. He opened the door and all of a sudden my whole body turned into dark red color with rage.

Doctor was really frightened by it and said, "Please, calm down and get in".

He asked me to sit and said "Yes, I had done a mistake but give me a chance, I will help you out from it. I will transplant your original skin to you, believe me".

"You son of a......... I already had put my life into a worst situation by believing you. I don't want to waste my time anymore. I will kill you and find an answer for it by myself", I said to frighten him.

"No, please don't do that. I beg you; I'll give you money which I offered you and transplant your skin back to you. Trust me", he requested.

I had no choice to move on except to accept it.

"Ok. If I find you cheating me again, then you can say good bye to this world", I said.

He asked me to stay at his house for today. And he was going to take me for the laboratory tomorrow.

"Why do we need to move there tomorrow? Start the procedure now", I spoke.

"I cannot be started now. I need to make arrangements for it. Please do understand my situation. It requires a perfect time and conditions to start it", he replied.

What can I do now, except listening to his foolish words. I just came to know about my situation 12 hours ago, that too not in a complete way.

I thought for a while "If I had rejected his offer, then I would have been dropping my customers in my taxi and would be waiting for my wages to receive. This is all because my greediness to that money offered by him". I just gave a serious look towards him.

"What is it for now?" he asked. I didn't reply to him.

"It's ok. Take rest. I will take you there in the morning", he said.

CHAPTER-9

ESCAPE PLAN

I was in a very deep sleep. Suddenly, I heard the sound of a glass broken. I just started moving to that place slowly hiding behind the wall. So that I can know what happened there. A group of doctors had assembled.

"You fool! Make your moves steadily. You are going to wake him up", doctor whispered.

Oh, my god! This doctor cheated me once again. He must have planned very big this time. I'm not going to spare him now. But, I need to know what's going on here first. I started to listen the conversation hiding behind the wall.

"Gentlemen, we are not going to lose him this time. My security guards will be reaching here within a short time. I have also arranged these shock sticks in case he becomes violent. Our creation must be applauded and we are going to use him as we wish, after hypnotizing him", Robert said with a cruel smile.

All these doctors started to applaud him; these cunning idiots had planned very well about using me. I won't let this happen. I'm going to finish it up before the security guards arrive here.

I just calmly stood in front of them and gave a look towards doctor. Doctor was speechless for a moment.

"A.......Adam still awake? We were discussing about the work of your transplantation", Robert said with a sort of fear in his tone.

"Doctor Robert, I heard everything you spoke", I said.

"Then what are you guys waiting for? Doctor's get him", Robert shouted.

Two doctors came running towards me. I had thrown chair on one of them and punched the other in his stomach. That scared all the other ones.

They started to run towards the entrance. I grabbed Dr.Robert collar and thrown him back.

"Others can leave", I shouted.

After seeing that bastards face, my skin tone changed its color which looked really frightening.

"Please, show mercy towards me. I am a fool. You gave me a chance, but my greediness made me like this. Leave me please, I beg you", doctor spoke in sad tone.

These words aren't enough to make me cool down. I gave a blow on his face. I couldn't control my anger and started punching him wherever I feel like. Blood started to flow from his mouth.

I thought for a while "Jesus! What am I doing? If I don't stop it, he will be dying". Suddenly, we heard the door knocking sound.

Doctor gave a smile and said, "It's over, Mr. Adam. Those are my security guards. Let's make a deal. You work for me; I will pay for it as much as you want".

This guy is never going to change. I replied him with a nasty kick on his chest; he flew through the window and landed outside his house.

I need to cross these guards now. So, there was nothing to think about. I just used the similar technique which helped me to cross the guards at the lab. I wore the doctor's suit and covered my hands with gloves, face with scarf and opened the door. The guards stared at me.

I said "Didn't you listen the big sound of a glass break? He is awake, go get him".

Those fools started running towards the room where I slept. I started to run towards my taxi which I parked at the corner of the street.

"There you go my lovely taxi" I screamed and drove back to my room.

If Mr.William finds the taxi outside of my house he is just going to take it away from me. So, I thought of parking it again in uncle's garage.

Uncle stared at me and asked the question which I expected "Who are you?"

"It's me Adam", I replied.

"What happened to your clothes?"

"Why did you wear these one?" he questioned me.

I just ignored him and moved quickly from there. I felt really bad for doing it. But, I don't have a choice.

CHAPTER-10

I FEEL LIKE "UNSTOPPABLE"

Professor Phil burg said me that there is only one way for me to get out of these, which is to find that doctor and make him to transplant my skin again. But, he is not in a situation to accept it. I have no option's left. So, it is better for me to get used to it.

I called Lisa and said, "It's over. I have to remain with this skin forever. Those doctors are never going to change. Once again they cheated me and I escaped from them".

Lisa remained silent for a moment and asked "So, what's your next move?"

"Do I have an option?" I replied.

She gave smile and said "Start living with it, you will feel better".

"I'm on it", I replied and ended the call.

I walked towards the mirror and gave a look. People will be scared if they see me with this skin. I need to cover my whole body. So, I need a jacket, scarf, steel-toed boots, aviator glasses, gloves etc. not even a part of my skin shouldn't be visible. I started walking across the street.

Everyone stared at me as it was a hot sunny day and I'm with those huge clothes on my body. The heat was immense and I am with these jackets, boots. I couldn't bare it and ran back to my room.

I removed everything and took a shower. These mornings seemed to be a hard time for me. So, I waited for the sun to set off.

Its 8p.m and I moved to the market to get the basic needs which are at the end of the street. I took the basket and finished filling it as fast as I can. Then, I moved to the bill counter to pay for it.

"Good evening, sir", he said.

I didn't reply him. He started to pick those items and stared at me for every 3 seconds.

"For God's sake, please don't stare at me and give me the bill", I screamed.

Everyone's attention was at me now. He billed my items. Within no time I gave him the money and left the market. It took me two hours to complete it.

I started walking towards my house and felt like someone was following me. Suddenly, four guys surrounded me with sharp knives in their hands.

"Just give us the money which you have and our job will be done without hurting you", said me of them.

I removed the gloves and said "I also have an option of kicking you people and walk away safely".

Those thugs started to laugh. Two guys are standing in front of me and the other two were behind me. I threw the items which I bought on their faces and punched the guys facing towards me. But the other two guys grabbed my legs from behind. I gave a push forward and those two guys caught my shoe this time. I gave another push and this time I escaped from their hands. But, they got my pair of shoes in their hands.

The other two grabbed my hands and threw me towards a building. I flew in the air and got hit with the building. I felt like falling off to the ground, but it didn't happen. My hands and legs got stuck to the wall. I started to climb the building. Those thugs got stunned of what they have seen. Even, I was also surprised for my act.

I thought for a while whether I was dreaming. But, I felt the pain on my chest when I was hit to the building. I climbed down the building.

"What are you man?" one of them asked.

"A super human", I replied.

I ran towards him and kicked on his chest with my knee. Other's started to run away from me. I picked up my stuff and moved towards my room. This time I gave a look whether anyone was watching me and climbed up of my house and screamed.

"THIS IS AWESOME!!!"

CHAPTER-11

SURPRISE FOR LISA

I need to share this incident with Lisa. So, I called her.

"Lisa, give me your exact location", I said.

"What!! Why do you need that for?" she enquired.

"It's really important thing to discuss with you. So, I need it", I replied.

"I'm at my friend's house which is at

120 west

106th street

New York", she replied.

I ended the call without saying a word and called my friend Danny [co-taxi driver]. Because it's too late and I don't want to disturb uncle for my taxi. Once again, he will be staring at me and I need to move out without replying him. To avoid all this stuff I called Danny.

"Danny! It's Adam", I said.

"Oh, man!! Where have you been? Boss is looking for you like a mad ass", he yelled.

"It's a long story man. But, I need your car as soon as possible. I'll explain it to you", I said.

"Ok. Meet me at the market. I'll give it to you", he said.

"Thanks bro", I replied and ended the call.

Danny was a close friend of mine. He was also frustrated to those rules of Mr.William. If I find a way out at the end, I will also retrieve Danny. I came back to my uniform again and walked towards the market. Danny was waiting for me and I explained everything for him.

"If you need any help, just give me a call bro. I'll break their bones", he squealed and left the place.

Finally, I reached her friend's house and parked my taxi at a distance to that house and thought to give a surprise to her.

I climbed up the house and searched through every window for her. At last, I found her. She was reading something. I called her.

She picked up the phone and said "Did you reach the place?"

"You need to do one thing now", I replied.

"OK. What am I supposed to do now?" she asked.

"Just stand from your position", I said.

"Ok. I stood, then what to do?" she enquired.

"Have patience Lisa, now walk towards the window," I replied.

"Oh, man. Now what?" she asked.

"Now open your window and say hi to Adam", I said.

She quickly opened her window and surprised by looking at me.

"Oh, man!! I don't know what to say. I thought it was a supernatural thing for humans to climb. But, at last I have seen it because of you", she said.

I gave a smile and explained her everything about the fight with those thugs. It wasn't a grilled window, so I sat on it with one leg in air and the other inside the room. She sat on a table beside the window and we both began to speak with each other.

The clock was running and we were speaking continuously about our daily life, her college incidents.

"So, what's your next move?" she asked me.

"It's........... I didn't plan it. If I get an idea by tomorrow, I'll implement it", I replied.

"Would you mind if I think about it and say to you?" she enquired.

"Are you kidding? You are the one who explained me about my situation and how can you believe that I am going to mind it?" I asked her.

She laughed and said, "That's ok. I take back my words".

"So......had a great talk with me?" I asked her.

"Yeah, indeed a great talk", she replied with a smile.

"Good night!!" I said and left the place.

"Be careful while you climb up the buildings. If anyone spots you, then you're gone", a voice came from behind.

I gave a smile to her and waved my hand. I called Danny to return his taxi. Otherwise, he is going to lose his wages if he not attends the pickups tomorrow. He drove me back to my house and advised me to be brave and move ahead. "Enough of adventures today and it's time for me to take rest" I thought and slept with a mind full of imagination.

CHAPTER-12

A GREAT INDIAN SCIENTIST

It was the call from Lisa which woke me up this time.

"Adam. I have got good news for you. Meet me at my college by 10a.m", she said.

"Oh, really!! So, you might have planned something bigger for my next move. I'll be there on time. See you at your college", I said and ended the call.

My phone began to ring again. I thought it would be Mr.William, but this time it was Uncle Patrick.

"Hello! Uncle. What's the matter?" I asked.

Uncle was crying and he didn't spoke a word.

"Please, speak uncle what's the problem?" I enquired.

"It's a sad news son. Doctor Robert died. I saw about it in today's newspaper", he replied.

How can this happen? I just stopped punching him after he started to bleed. I questioned myself.

"Be brave uncle. I'll drop you at his funeral", I said.

"No son. The funeral was completed yesterday", he said.

"I'm really sorry. I would have taken you there, if it was known to me earlier", I apologized.

"It's ok Adam. Just I felt like sharing it with you and said it", he said and ended the conversation.

I quickly ran towards the door to get the newspaper. It was written he died due to an accident and he was hit by a car. The location was just outside his house.

Now, I got everything clear in my mind. After, I kicked him on his chest he flew through the window and landed outside his house where a car might have hit him and he died due to it.

Thank god! For saving me from a murder case. Otherwise, cops might be chasing me now.

Oops! I forgot about my appointment which I gave to Lisa. I rushed towards my taxi. I asked uncle for the keys and maintained the same silence again with him.

I drove my taxi to her college. She was waiting for me. I walked towards her. She gave me a hug and took me to her professor's room.

The professor was speaking with someone. Lisa introduced me to that person.

"He is Mr.Ashok and he is from India", Lisa said.

"Glad to meet you, sir. My name is Adam", I introduced about myself.

"He is also a zoologist, but more over a crazy scientist. He links the animal life with our daily needs and usage. This time his crazy thing worked for you".

"He designed a fabric cloth which can change its color according to the thing which it is in contact with. So, you can just move across the streets with it maintaining a constant color on it", Lisa said.

I felt like "No more jackets, no more toed shoes. I am a free bird now".

"It's a remarkable invention, sir. You made me a free bird now. It is really going to help me", I said.

He gave me the suit. I began to wear it with all the eyes on me. It's just like a skin tight dress with four pieces. [Face mask, gloves, shirt, and pant]. It covered my entire body, but I need a contact to absorb the color. He made holes so that I can touch the floor with my feet.

The flooring was white in color. Slowly, my body turned its color to white then the suit changed its color.

All the three applauded.

"It's working sir. Thank you, so much", I said.

I wore my shoe and suddenly my suit turned to black color.

I took Lisa out of the room and asked "Who is going to pay for it?"

"He is my professor's friend. So, he understood your situation and designed it for you. Now no need of formalities like thanking him. He is already tired off after designing it. So, he needs rest", Lisa said.

"At least, I can thank you for listening such a sweet words from you", I said to Lisa.

"Do you feel that those two words are going to satisfy me?" she asked.

"I guess no. Then what do you need me to do for you?" I asked.

"Pick me up at my friend's house and take me out for dinner tonight", she said.

It was like a combo offer for me to cheer first was the suit and the other was dinner with Lisa.

"I have a suit to wear now. So, I can fly with you anywhere", I said.

She gave a diagonal look towards me and laughed.

"I'll pick you up at sharp 8:00p.m. See you", I said and left the place.

CHAPTER-13

DELIGHT FULL DINNER

Dinner with the girl whom I loved the most. That was the right situation which I was waiting for to propose her. I don't know what sort of answer I was going to receive from her but one thing is clear that I truly love her.

It was around 7:30 PM now. So, I started my taxi to her home. I became very punctual due to those unwanted rules of William. So, I was in time at her house.

I sounded the horn, she opened the door slowly and I was speechless for a moment.

She was looking gorgeous in her dress. It was a black one with a matching wallet and also a hat. I opened the door for her and she sat inside the car.

"You look beautiful today", I said.

She gave me a smile and asked "Is it today or every day?"

I laughed and started the taxi straight to mandarin hotel.

I didn't even spoke a word during the drive because my mind was thinking about the answer from her.

Finally, we reached the hotel and moved inside. I already had reserved a table for us. We sat and I passed the menu card for her to order.

She ordered it and gave a strange look towards me.

"What?" I asked.

"You are behaving a little strange today. I don't seem you giving work to your mouth much", she said.

I just gave a smile and said, "No. Not like that. Everything is fine."

She just nodded her head and the food was ready for us to start.

I remained silent until we ate the food and left the hotel. She became really sad for my behavior and that was the situation I was waiting for to start my act.

"Lisa, close your eyes. I am going to tie this hand kerchief over your eyes. Don't even try to remove them until I say", I said.

At last, I got a smile on her face and tied it. She sat in the car and I drove the car straight towards a building where I can perform it.

I opened the car door and asked her to come with me.

"Lisa, now hug me tight and don't remove the hanky", I said.

She hugged me and I started climbing the building.

"Oh, my god! Where are you taking me?" she screamed.

"Be patient. Everything will be clear for you", I said.

She loved the climbing thing the most. So, I planned my act in this way.

"Now, remove it and open your eyes", I said.

She slowly removed the hanky and was stunned to figure out what just happened.

"This is really awesome. I didn't even imagine it. Thanks a lot. You really surprised me", She said.

"I LOVE YOU", I said.

She remained silent for few seconds and said, "That was the thing I was expecting from you today. I LOVE YOU too".

I was not able to figure out whether it was a dream or not. Lisa loved me too.

I climbed down slowly without making any harm to her. The silence still remained between us. I did not know what to speak the next thing with her. She was just smiling looking towards me.

I dropped Lisa back at her house and returned to my home dreaming about her.

CHAPTER-14

PROBLEMS FOR SCIENTIST

Everything was going fine till then, but suddenly I got a phone call which made things even worse for me. It was an unknown number.

"Hello!" I said.

"Adam! It's a bit of emergency you need to come to my house immediately", the person on the phone call said.

"Yeah, it's ok. I will come but, can I first know who is it?" I asked him.

"It's me, Ashok. I was the one who gave you the suit", he said.

"Ok, sir. Can I know what is it about?" I questioned.

"You idiot, I would have told you if I meant to, but I need to show you and tell you something. Now, please stop your question part and arrive here as quickly as possible", he replied me with aggression.

"Stay right there, sir. I will drive as fast as I can to reach you home. But, one last question. Please, don't fire on me. Where is your house located?" I enquired with a lowest tone.

"Oh, man.

1220 3rd Avenue

New York.

Now, please end the call and drive here straight away", he said and ended the call.

These science people are losing their patience day by day. First of all, they need to invent something to increase it. Thank god, Lisa was better of all the science people whom I have met.

Oh, my god! I need to tell about this Ashok's call to Lisa now. So, I called her.

"Hello, superhuman!! What's the matter?" she asked.

"What kind of superman? I am facing huge problems for every step ahead. I feel exhausted with this thing", I replied.

"Sir, what's the problem now?" she asked.

"The person who gave me the suit had called me and asked me to meet him at his house now. I need you to come along with me to his house", I replied.

"Is it? Then it must have been an important thing. So, we need to get there immediately. Pick me up at the same place. Drive fast, I'll be waiting. And last thing. Don't forget to suit up", she said with a smile and stopped the conversation.

I imagined that the doctor's advice of testing drug on me would change my fate. Really, it had changed my life a lot with an upgraded level of fate. Even, god must have been trying to figure out a solution for my problem.

I had no option. If I try to open up then I'll be in the museum and all people will be staring at me every day. Those are all never ending thoughts in my mind until I return back to the old Adam with human skin.

I cannot even do those monkey climbing's in the public. If I do so, they will capture me and follow my way all along to my house.

I started driving to Lisa's house and this time Danny called me.

"Bro, I need to talk to you", Danny said.

"I'm in a busy thing right now. Catch you in the evening buddy", I said.

"That's ok, bro. see you", he said and ended the call.

Lisa was waiting for me. She gave a smile and opened the door to sit.

"Hola superhuman. Everything will be fine. Stay cool", she said.

"Hope so", I said and started driving.

"What might have happened out there?" I asked her.

"I don't have any idea. I think there might be a problem in your suit", she replied.

Those words shocked me. I suddenly applied brakes.

"Are you kidding? My situation would become even horrible now", I said.

She began to laugh and said "Just imagine. You are walking in the middle of the street and your suit stops working and become transparent".

Her laughing was extremely hard. I just kept quiet and started to drive.

"Ok. I was just kidding. There's no defect in your suit. He just certified it in front of me. I really don't know what he is going to tell", she said.

"Fine", I replied

"Now don't put an angry look on your face and give a smile at me", she said.

"I am wearing a mask and how come you can see my smile?" I asked.

"Laugh aloud. I have my ears to hear it", she said.

"OK, fine. This is for you", I said and imitated her laugh.

"I asked you to laugh, not to duplicate my smile", she said with a little aggression in her voice.

"So, Lisa's brain is sharp enough to catch my smile", I said.

She began to beat me with a smile. Finally, we reached his house and moved towards the entrance. I knocked the door.

"It's open. Come in", a voice came.

We moved inside and everything was misplaced and scattered in his house.

"Oh, Jesus. What happened here? Why everything is scattered?" I asked him.

"The blueprint of your suit had been stolen", he said.

"Oh, no. this is an unexpected one. Did anyone notice him entering the house?" I asked him.

"I just asked my neighbors about this. They said that they couldn't trace him out as he covered up his entire body", he replied.

"What is he going to do with it? It is going to suit for me only", I asked.

"He can modify it and sell it for million dollars. I didn't inform anyone about this suit because it doesn't benefit you if I open it up to everyone", he replied.

"Then we need to trace him out and stop him before he sells it", Lisa said.

"Ok, But how are we going to catch him?" I asked.

"Shall we inform the cops!" he asked.

"No. No. Don't do that. If you inform them, then they are going to check your recent calls and visits to interrogate. If it happens then they will trace me out too. They will be finding that suit with me and also they will know about my skin. All the hard work which I am doing to survive will be in vain. So, please don't do that stupid thing", I said. "we will figure out another way to find him and surely we are going to catch them".

"Indeed a good thought. But, we need to figure out as fast as we can", Ashok said.

We began to discuss about the plans and ways to catch him and everything seemed not at all good. We all were tired off thinking about it.

Lisa said that she will prepare lunch for us. I was eager to eat the food prepared by her. She served it and I really loved the food. Even Ashok was also very much impressed by her tasty food.

I said him that we will be leaving now and asked him to call if he traces him.

But, one thing was running in my mind. The suit thing was known only to four of us. But, he figured his house and stole only that blueprint. Something seemed not at all good here. There must be a use for him; that is why he might have targeted it.

I said bye to Mr.Ashok and left his house with Lisa.

"So, where are you moving now?" she asked me.

"I need to meet my friend Danny now. He said that he needs to talk to me", I replied.

"Alright! Does he know about your super human thing?" she asked.

"Yeah, he knows. I said him and even showed it to him", I replied her.

"Ok, then move on", she said.

I dropped Lisa at her house and called Danny to come to my house.

He reached within no time and I moved there.

We both moved into my house.

"Hi, bro. What was the thing about?" I asked him.

"It's a good news for you. I explained everything happened to you to William. I felt that he would be informing all these to the cops. But, to my surprise he felt sad for you and asked you to join the work, after everything gets settled. And he also asked to say him if you need any help", Danny replied.

"That's really good news to cheer up. Even Mr.William does have a kind heart except that bloody doctor. It is all because of him", I said.

"Chill bro. I need to move now. There's some work left for me to do", Danny said.

"That's ok. You can leave now. Thanks for that good news. Catch you again?" I said and he left the place.

CHAPTER-15

WORK FOR COPS

Those sweet words from Danny gave me a sleep with mind free of thoughts. But, I was afraid of what sort of news am I going to listen today. I was prepared for it as it became a hobby for me.

Is this the way a super human need to live his life? I was getting a sort of feel to use this power to earn some money. But, I slapped my face and thought that already my life turned upside down due to that greediness towards money. If I continue it, there will be nothing left.

I took the newspaper and the very first heading was "Burglar's attack the city". I started reading it.

It was written that the cops could not trace down the thief as they broke the surveillance camera before the robbery and also they performed robbery without leaving any clues behind. And another interesting thing is that every robbery was performed in the similar fashion.

This is indeed a breaking news. It was the first time ever that this intelligence team has said that they couldn't figure out a clue. Probably, they might get it from the further investigation.

The before day there was a robbery even at Mr.Ashok's house. But, everything was scattered there and also there was no camera to trace him out. So, the thief might be a different one who robbed the blue print. It was quiet interesting that he performed the robbery perfectly.

I feel like helping them out but they are going to raise me hundred questions about my story, if I go there. But, I need to know about the situation of what happened exactly out there and get the clues. So I called Lisa for it.

"Hello, Lisa. Did you get the news?" I asked her.

"Yeah, I just came to know about it. That's quite a tricky thing. Robberies all around the city within a night. He might have planned it perfectly", she replied me.

"I need you to move there and find out what's happening?" I asked her.

"What!!! Are you mad? How are they going to allow me inside and say me everything about what happened out there", she replied with a tone of seriousness.

"I have a plan for you. Cops over there must have assembled a group of witnesses to solve the case. You need to join among them", I said.

"Oh, my god!! What should I speak there; they are going to ask me hundreds of questions. No, I am not fit for it. Just leave me", she said.

"You are going to speak with those witnesses first, about what they have found strange in the bank and question them accordingly. You need to say that you have also noticed the same thing to the cops", I said.

"How come you think that they are going to answer me? They are strangers you idiot. Find someone else for it. If I get caught doing it, then I will be in prison for doing it. I am a science student and not at all good at these things Mr. Adam", she shouted.

"Use your sharp brain Lisa, you can easily communicate with them. Just plug-in your Bluetooth until you reach the interrogation and just remove it while you enter. I'll be there to help you. I won't let it go easily", I said to her.

She was silent for a while and asked "Do you feel that I am going to complete it successfully?"

"You are the one who perfectly suits for it. That is why I called you to do it. Now move ahead and complete your task", I motivated her

"I am moving there keeping belief in you. If I get caught, then the first name I am going to reveal is you and your super human thing", she said.

I laughed and said "Ok. That's fine. Now move there and give me a call".

She moved to that place and plugged her Bluetooth.

"Lisa, first make a look around and see whether any news reporters are speaking with the witnesses", I said.

"Yeah, I found one", she replied.

"That's good. Now move towards him and look for any two to three things which he spells out", I asked her.

She moved towards him and he was saying that everything was normal until the bank is closed and the cops asked to figure out the faces.

"Lisa, now move towards a cop and say him that you are a witness and you can figure out the faces", I said.

She moved towards a cop and said the same thing.

He asked her to come with him and she removed the Bluetooth from her ears. I was really worried about what might have happened there.

They will be showing Lisa the faces of all people who entered the bank the day before. So, she needs to figure out. If she randomly guesses one face, then they will be interrogating her about the strange acts which the person had made.

If she fails to say, they will be checking whether she had attended the bank or not on that day. That's it.

They will come to know that she was pretending and they are going to scare her to get the name of who asked her to do it which was me. I need to plan something different again to escape it.

This time I need to face the cops, which is a very big task for me to complete. It is never easy with those fellows.

What if she says that she didn't find the face among them? That could be a better one for her to choose. Then they will be asking her contact details and if possible they will be dropping Lisa at her house for supporting them.

Jesus! At least do me a favor this time. Bring her out safely.

It became more than an hour since she ended the call. Thoughts started to run again in my mind.

This time it was about the escape plan. They are not going to leave Lisa until they found me. So, it would be better if I surrender myself to them and explain them everything that happen to me since the past few weeks.

So, I started to drive towards the bank for a face off. If Lisa comes out safely without any obstacles, then I will drop her and plan further. If Lisa comes out with a darkest situation then I'll surrender and make her free.

I drove to that place and waited for her at a little distance from the bank.

CHAPTER-16

SITUATIONS GETTING EVEN HARDER

There she is coming out of the bank. She was surrounded by three cops and they all were suited up with heavy guns. The cops might have taken the issue seriously about these robberies.

The reporters started to surround her and began to ask questions. She was responding to them with a saddest expression. I was not able to figure out why for she was sad.

The cops left her and she was free now. She started to walk away from those reporters and called a taxi. I thought she might be calling me after reaching her house.

I followed that taxi. To my surprise, she did not go to her home. Instead she moved to the seaside and sat on a bench out there. She was really feeling sad about something. I parked my taxi and moved towards her to speak. She didn't even give a look at my face.

I sat beside her and asked "What happened out there? Why didn't you call me?"

She remained silent without answering to me.

"For god's sake, please speak to me Lisa. I am very much worried about you", I screamed at her.

"Ok. Listen now. I just moved inside and they asked me few questions about that thief. I said them the same thing which we planned. They showed me the pictures of the people who entered the bank on that day. And that's where, I found you in those pictures", she said.

"What!!! I was at home after I left you", I said.

"You just said that you are going to meet Danny. So, why were you at the bank?" she asked me.

"I called Danny to meet me at my house and he was with me at my house. I am not able to understand what the hell you are speaking", I offended her.

"The suit was present only with you and it doesn't fit to anyone else. Is this the reason you sent me there for an escape plan?" she questioned me in an incensed way.

"How do I need to explain you? I was not the one out there. Someone might have copied my dress. Oh, no wait a minute. Professor's friend said that his blueprint was stolen", I said.

"Ok. So what?" she asked.

"The fellow at the bank had suited just like me. So, my guess was wrong. He is the same thief who robbed both the places and many other banks", I replied.

She began to think for a few moments.

"So, it was not you in the bank last evening. I'm really sorry. I didn't even think about it. I have a dumb brain. Please, forgive me for all those words", she said sadly.

"It's not your fault. Anyone who might have seen that picture would have doubted me. What did you just say? The suit is not going to fit for anyone", I yelled.

"I didn't say it. But, yes human skins have almost only two to three colors. So, when it gets contact to person out there was having a black colored suit", she answered me.

"That means, there is one more person out there having a similar skin like me", I screamed.

I didn't even imagine about this thing, one more person like me. So, the doctor created one more human with a chameleon skin.

"Adam. Is this thing never going to end? We are finding hurdles on every path", she said with a surprised tone.

"Did you tell the cops anything about the guy in that picture?" I asked her with a fearful voice.

"No, I just said them that I could not find him and walked out, thinking that it was you", she replied.

Thank god, otherwise the cops might be chasing me now. If he start robberies in the entire city and leave a little clue there. Then, these cops are going to catch me instead of him. I need to trace him out as quickly as possible and put an end to him.

"Lisa, I don't know what to say. But, we need to catch him before he robs the other banks and shops. If it won't happen then I will be in danger", I said.

"Ok, but how?" she yelled.

"I don't know. We are going to just move forward and find answers for them", I replied.

The person in the suit might have accepted to that doctor's agreement to do whatever he says. That is why, he is robbing the banks. But, the doctor is dead.

So, he can gather as much money he wants and there is no need to share the money since the doctor is dead.

"I have to say this thing to Mr.Ashok now", I said to Lisa.

"Yes, tell him that his property was found in a burglar's hand with a similar skin of you", Lisa said.

"Everything is cleared, right?" I asked her.

"About what?" she in return asked me.

"What else are you going to expect me to ask you? About those things which you thought that, I was the thief at the bank", I replied angrily.

She gave me a smile and said "I apologized already to you about it. But, you are starting it again. I'm going to kill you this time. Let's move now".

I drove Lisa back to her house and called Mr.Ashok.

"Sir, the blueprint which was stolen from you is in a burglar's hand. He built a new suit and one more shocking thing is that he is having a skin similar to me", I said.

He surprised and said, "Oh, really! Then you will be in danger by his moves. Be careful, Adam. One wrong step and your hard work to save yourself will be lost".

Those words made me to frighten.

"Sure, sir. I'm on it", I said and ended the call.

I am in need of money right now. So, I asked Danny to lend me. He said that he will give me them in the evening. So, I need to wait for him now at my house.

CHAPTER-17

MEETING DANNY

I heard the sound of someone knocking my door. I was waiting for that person and opened the door.

"Hey! Adam", Danny screamed and hugged me.

"Hi, bro", I said with a sorrow tone.

"Is everything fine?" he questioned me.

"Everything seemed to be fine, but nothing is good here", I spoke sadly.

"What's the matter buddy?" Danny questioned me.

"I came to know that the doctor transplanted the skin not only for me, but also to another guy. He stole the blueprint of that suit and started robbing the banks with that suit", I answered with sort of unhappiness.

"Jesus! I am not able to imagine your situation. You are producing a surprise for me, whenever I meet you", Danny yelled.

"But, these are the things that are happening to me daily. I feel like revealing myself to the world. I don't even know what they are going to do after I show them", I said.

"Ooooo!! That's not going to help you then. It turns out to be a 50:50 chance for you. If they cure it then there will be a problem. But, if they fail you will be treated like an alien out there. My suggestion is to stay calm for few days and find another way to get out of this shit", Danny advised me.

"That is all what I had to do right now Danny", I said to him.

"That's good. You asked me for the money. How much do you need?" Danny asked.

"How much did you get?" I asked him.

"$500", Danny replied.

"Give me half of that and I'll return you as soon as possible", I said.

"No need to worry bro. Give them back with your convenience", Danny said,

I smiled and asked, "So, how is your daily work going on?"

"It's the same filthy stuff. Extra work, cutting down of wages everything is exactly the same including Williams", he said.

We both began to laugh and he said that he need to pick up someone. So, he rushed out of my house.

I started to think about my next step which is to get hold of that thief and break his legs.

CHAPTER-18

UNCLE HELPS ME OUT

I couldn't sleep as my thinking was on, about my next move. So, I need to trace that stranger now. The doctor might have transplanted his skin at the same place where it was done for me.

But, the place might be guarded and locked as well. So, how do I get in there? Oh, no! I need to beat those security guards again. Instead, I can plan something different.

Uncle is a close friend of doctor. I can expect a little information about that lab from him. Do I need to hide my skin from uncle? Or tell him everything. This is the next thing which I need to prepare for. He is an old man; will he be able to digest the truth?

Many more questions started to run in my mind. I will meet him tomorrow morning and move according to the situation. This made me a little relaxed and I started trying to sleep again.

I did not close my curtain properly. There was a gap of about 5 to 6cm. So, the sun rays passed through the window and fell right on my eyes. I woke up and took a shower.

I drove my taxi straight to his house. The door was locked from inside. I knocked it. He is an old man. So, it took time for him to move towards the door and open it.

I can do nothing instead of waiting for him to open the door. He did not recognize me as I was in my suit, which covered my entire body.

"Yes, what do you need?" he asked me.

"It's me Adam. I need to talk to you uncle", I replied.

"What happened to you? What's the matter with your outfit?" he questioned me.

"I'll explain everything to you. Let's please, sit and talk", I said.

"Ok. Ok. Get in son", uncle said.

We slowly started to move towards his room. I moved to the kitchen to get some water for uncle.

"Thank you, Adam", he said and drank it.

"Adam, now tell me. What's the matter?" he asked.

I didn't know where to start. So, I just removed the face mask.

"Jesus! What happened to your face?" uncle screamed.

I removed my hand gloves and he gave another scream and started walking towards me to observe my skin.

"Adam, I don't know what to say. What's all this? Please speak to me", uncle yelled.

It's time for me to tell the truth for uncle.

"This happened a few weeks ago. When you asked me to get your reports from the doctor, he offered me something which changed my entire life," I said.

"What did he offer?" uncle asked.

"He wanted my body to test the drug on me. I rejected it first. But my stinginess to earn more money made me to take that offer", I said.

"Oh, no! Adam, this is indeed a big mistake", uncle said.

If I say the truth that the doctor had cheated me, then the uncle will not be able to digest the news. Since, Doctor Robert was his dearest friend.

"The drug which he tested on me had shown negative effect on me. To compensate it the doctor changed my skin to a suitable one. This was the thing happened out there", I lied him.

Uncle remained calm for some time.

"Past is past. My friend is no more. Did you find any treatment for this thing?" Uncle enquired.

"I'm on it. But…….." I sighed.

"Do you want to ask something?" Uncle questioned.

"I need some more details about that drug thing. They are present at that laboratory. But the place is guarded and lab is locked. Can you help me to get them?" I asked.

"About a year ago, I was sick and my condition was very serious. I moved to this doctor's hospital. He treated me for about 2 weeks and after my discharge, the doctor asked me to come with him to his lab. So, I moved with him. You need a key code to enter the lab", uncle said.

I become very attentive and asked, "A key code!! Yes!! That's the thing. Do you know anything about it?"

"You are a lucky one. I noticed the key, when he entered it", uncle said.

"I was waiting to hear those words from your mouth. Please, tell them", I requested.

Uncle gave a smile and said, "It's 1413. But, I cannot help you to cross the guards out there".

"Leave it to me. I'll handle them. Thank you, so much uncle for the key code", I said.

Uncle threw a smile on my face again.

"I need to move now. Take care. Bye!!" I said and left the place to drive straight towards Lisa's house. Because, there is something which she needs to do.

I reached the place and sounded the horn. She came running inside the house as if she was expecting my visit to her house.

"I know you would come" Lisa said.

"At least, today I felt that everything was normal. But, you produced me a surprise. How did you know?" I asked.

"It's a simple guess. I knew you will be planning your next move by today's morning and you need my help to implement it. That's it", she said.

I started staring at her but she was laughing heavily.

"Ok. Your brain's working fine today. But, listen I got the key to enter the lab, where we can get the information about that burglar. But, there's a problem it is guarded", I said.

"So, half of our job is done and rest half did you plan it?" she asked.

"I need Danny to do something for us", I said.

"Ok. Here you go, you planned the rest half of it. So, make him to do it", she said.

I called Danny and said "Hey, Danny. I got some work for you. I want you to forge an ID card of a reporter and get a mike and camera from him. Meet me at Edson square with them".

"Ok, bro. You'll get them", Danny said and ended the call.

"You look strange with that mike thing as a reporter", Lisa said.

"That is why I choose you to do it", I said with a smile.

"No. No. Not me again. I cannot risk every time. I'm not fit for it", Lisa begged.

"Don't worry. I'll be there with you. Now calm down and let me finish my task", I said.

I started driving to the Edson square. Lisa's face looked much more beautiful with a feel of tension on her face. I was enjoying it.

I found Danny and asked him to get in. I drove my car straight away to the lab. Danny gave me the ID card which I asked Lisa to wear.

"Lisa, prepare some questions about the death of the doctor, which you need to ask those guards over there and Danny hold that camera to start shooting it. I hope the scene is clear to you. You need to distract those guards from there and I move inside for that information", I said.

Both of them nodded their heads as they were not in a position to speak.

I parked the taxi at a distance to that lab and sent both these people towards them. It seemed to be a good plan for me as the lab is situated outside the city. I could just see them.

This time I did not give Lisa the Bluetooth as I need to handle myself and search those things, so as not to make the scene clumsy. I left her with Danny out there.

Lisa began to speak with a security guard. I viewed them through my binoculars. There were only three guards to my surprise.

But, I can see only two of them speaking with her. I ran towards the lab through the back path and threw a stone in heap of grass present there to distract that remaining guard, present at the entrance.

He did not move but gave a look at that place. I threw a stone again, this time he moved from there. I rushed towards the entrance and entered the key code.

I moved inside the room adjacent to the one in which they ruined me. To my surprise, my guess was correct. There were some instruments present in that room which they used on me. I started to check the cupboards, tables, everywhere to get it. At last, I found it.

I have no time to check the details of that burglar there. So, I just took the file and moved towards the entrance. I entered the key code and moved outside.

The guard whom I distracted has seen me from a distance. I ran towards him and gave a blow on his face before he screams out. I covered him with the same heap which distracted him. I moved towards my taxi and signaled them to end the drama and come back.

They came to the taxi within no time; I drove straight to my room as fast I can without having a look at that file. We reached the room and closed the door. We sat on chairs and opened the file. To our surprise, there was no picture of his face on it. There was only about his details.

"Douglas Estate

26 west

17th street

New York."

At last, we have something to cheer.

"Danny can you please have a look at that location?" I asked.

"Sure. I'll call you after reaching that place", he said and moved from my house.

CHAPTER-19

LAST HOPE

Lisa and I were waiting for the call from Danny. I did not move to that place to get him, as he might recognize me easily and escape from there immediately. Danny will be tracing him secretly and call me. Then, I'll figure out rest of the part which is to break his neck.

"It's almost done buddy. Stay cool now", Lisa said.

"I'm in a state where I don't know how to stay cool", I said.

Lisa laughed and said "So, the super humans are facing hard times these days. Don't worry, Adam. You too will find a good time one day".

"Really!! Check out my situation from the starting. Did you find any good time?" I asked her.

"No……. but, you may find from now", Lisa replied.

"Leave it. I don't even have a hope that I can get good days. I was tortured by Mr.William in those days and now by this doctor thing. Life's a hell for me", I said with an intense emotion in my voice.

Lisa placed my hand into her hands and said, "Believe me. Now or the other day everything will be finished and you will feel better then".

Those words seemed really touching for me and boosted me x5 times.

My phone rang. It was Danny.

"Danny, did you find him?" I asked immediately.

"The door is locked Adam. I'm sorry. I couldn't figure him out", Danny replied.

"Oh, man!! Did you ask the people around his house or his neighbors of his where about?" I enquired.

"Yeah, I did it too. They said that the house was locked since 2 months. So, no one entered it", Danny replied.

"Danny stay right at that place. I'm coming there. I need to find at least something about him", I said and ended the call.

"Are we moving to that place?" Lisa questioned.

"Yes, sweet heart. Let's move", I said and started the taxi.

"Did he mention the wrong address in that file?" Lisa asked.

"To my guess, it is the right one because the doctor won't produce any type of faulty proofs in that lab. He might be staying away from that house after the transplantation, to secure himself", I said.

"Your brain is working sharp enough now", Lisa said with a smile on her face.

"But, I'm not sure whether we will be able to trace him in that location or not. His moves are sharp enough and unpredictable", I said.

"So, is there no way to catch him", Lisa said.

"Every thief makes at least one mistake which we need to figure out. I'm waiting for that chance", I spoke with intensity.

We reached that place and Danny was waiting for me at the corner of that street. I moved towards his house secretly and checked it again. It's locked and if we try to break it, then it sounds an alarm which alerts the cops and my entire plan will be ruined.

"Danny we need to watch these streets carefully for at least 3-4 days. We may find him. Let's give it a try", I said to him.

"Ok, bro. But……. Let's do it", Danny said.

"What happened do you have a problem?" I asked.

"No. nothing, just I thought about my pickups. But, I'll manage it. Not a big issue for me", Danny said.

"That's good to listen from you bro. Thank you, so much. I'll drop Lisa back at her house and join you", I said and left the place.

We reached her house.

"I have troubled you a lot and made you to face many problems. You spent most of the time with me in spite of that college. I have only one thing to say other than all of this. That is I LOVE YOU more than anything else in the world. And I'm here to do anything for you", I spoke.

She gave me a hug and said, "That is why I am doing everything for you to survive. I love you too. Take care", she said and went outside.

I drove back to that place. Danny and I watched every person in that street. But, we couldn't trace him down. We continued it for more than a week. There were no robberies in the city after the big one. But, we did not lose the hope and watched for him as this is our last way to find him.

CHAPTER-20

AN UNKNOWN CALL

We got tired of that searching job and returned back to our houses. We had kept an eye on every corner of that street. Surprisingly, we did not find any other clue other than this house.

What's the use? It's locked and if we try to break it, cops are going to catch us. Days are passing but we could not find him. Danny almost gave up and asked me to come back and join the work. That's not the thing I really wanted.

I suffered fair enough to get rewarded. I cannot leave this thing in the middle. I am fed up with that routine life and I cannot start my taxi work again. Lisa also had almost given up. But, her words are still running in my mind to wait for the good times. She almost sacrificed one month of her research for me. I cannot remain silent in this way.

I need to implement something better than the previous one. This is the way I am living these days with my brain full of thoughts. What to do? Where to start? Is it going to succeed?

It is a fine evening. I made coffee for myself. At least, a coffee can cool up my mind. What!!! Superhuman cools his mind with a cup of coffee? A superhuman is also a "human" at last.

I heard the sound of my phone ring. I thought the call might be from Lisa. But, this time it was an unknown number.

"Hello! Who is it?" I asked.

I didn't get the answer for it. I repeated it again. There was no answer again.

"For god's sake, please speak man", I said.

"Cool down, Adam!! I know you might be tired off in search of me", the stranger said.

"You son of a ……!!! Stop hiding from me. I knew you were tracking us", I said.

The stranger laughed and said, "So, finally you came to know about that thing".

"Why the hell are you doing all these things?" I asked.

"I'm enjoying it. See, we are different from others. Take advantage of it man. Don't be a fool", he said.

"Now stop offering me. The one who first offered this thing is no more. It's your turn to die now", I said.

"Oh!!! Cool down, Mr. Adam. Your imagination may not become true always. You were not the one who killed doctor", stranger said.

"What!!! Is the accident true then?" I asked.

"Of course. Because my plan is never going to fail", he replied.

"You scoundrel, so you killed Doctor Robert", I said.

He gave a wild laugh and said "After you pushed him from the window, I hit him with my car and left the place".

"Why did you kill him? He was the one who modified you. Didn't you feel any sense of respect for him?" I asked with a loud tone.

"I am not here to entertain or share my money. So, he is useless for me. He might create a problem for me in future like informing my details to cops. So, I eliminated everyone of that doctor's team", he replied.

"Jesus!! You are a disgrace to human kind. Now, what do you want from me?" I asked.

"Ok. You got the point. It's simple. Join with me in the robberies. We can become billionaires. There will be no one to stop us. Let's benefit this thing man. Use your brain at least now", he replied.

"Really!! Get lost. I could have done it, if I wish to do those atrocious things. I am already fed up with this thing, now I cannot create new problems for myself", I said.

"I have killed four people; you are not a big deal for me. I can eliminate even you, if you want it", he said.

"I'll be waiting. That's what the thing I want, you meet me and I'll kill you", I spoke which kept him silent for a moment.

"That's great to hear from you Mr. Adam. Don't let your confidence go down. You will be meeting me soon enough. Be prepared", he said.

"I thank you for that advice. You really motivated me. Be prepared to die", I replied sarcastically.

"You forgot the thing that you need to face problems if you reject my offer", he said.

"What!!! Are you kidding? Why should I?" I asked.

I did not get the reply.

"Hello….."

"Hello….. Tell me", I said.

He ended the call with that sentence. What did he mean by it? I need to face problems, if I reject to join him. What sort of problems? He left it for me to think it. Oh, god!!! Not again.

CHAPTER-21

MEETS CHIEF OF POLICE

"You need to face problems even if you reject my offer".

That's the thing he left for me. Did he mean that he is going to kill me? No, it's not the thing because he already said that he will kill me. Then, what it might be?

Oh, no!!! What if he makes a robbery and leaves a clue behind about me? The cops will undoubtedly arrest me and he can rob the rest easily.

I cannot let this happen. But, how do I stop it? No, one's going to believe my story. If he leaves a clue, then there's no chance for me to escape.

So, only option for me is to inform the cops about this thing. I called Danny.

"Danny, I need to meet the chief of police right now", I said.

"Are you mad? It's a rubbish thing to meet him. You will be caught instead of that burglar", Danny yelled.

"Don't panic. I have a plan to deal with him. Tell me how can I meet or contact him", I said.

"It's not easy to meet him. Moreover, situations became critical for them due to those lootings", Danny said.

"Ok, bro. I'll take care of it. Thanks for the info", I said and ended the call.

I am not in a position to keep on thinking. I drove my taxi straight to his office. I could do nothing except this to save myself in this limited time, hoping that he believes me and finds a solution for this unsolved question.

I parked my taxi and walked straight away inside. One of those cops stopped me.

"What do you want? Why did you mask your face?" he asked.

"I know the one who is responsible for all these burglaries. Please, let me speak to the chief of police about this thing. It's an emergency thing", I said.

He called him and said, "Sir, we have a problem. A guy has come here saying that he knows the person who robbed the banks".

"Ok", he said and ended the call.

"Sir, please cooperate with us we need to interrogate you", he said.

"Sure, but I will speak only to him", I said.

"To whom?" he enquired.

"To the chief of police", I said.

"Ok. Follow me", he said and took me to the interrogation room.

"Sit down here and wait for him to come", he said.

The room was quite frightening. There was only one light which was fit above my head and four surveillance cameras are present at the four corners of the room. One side of the room was fit with a glass, which is visible only from the other side.

He entered and sat in front of me.

"So, who is that guy?" was the very first question the chief of police asked me.

"I don't know his name but he wears the something which I wore know", I said.

"What!!! Keep a thing in mind that you are dealing with the cops and answer me perfectly", he ordered.

"This is a special kind of suit. It does take the same color which your skin is going to have. He stole that blueprint from my friend and designed it himself. This suit thing is going to work for me and him", I said.

"So, you want to say that you have a black skin now", he said.

These guys are not going to believe me. So, I removed my mask. He jumped out of his chair.

"What happened for your skin? Are you a human?" he asked fearfully.

"Yes, I am a human. But, one doctor made this to me and also to that guy. He not only robbed the banks, but also killed that doctor and his team", I said.

"This is terrible man. It's highly impossible", he said and touched my skin.

I remained calm; he began to observe me for few minutes.

"We don't have time sir. You need to catch him immediately before he robs the other banks. He is highly dangerous", I said.

"How can I believe you? I need to interrogate you further", he asked.

"I'll prove it. Just show me the video footage of the bank before the robbery", I said.

He took me to another room where he showed me the footage.

"Stop! There he is, zoom it a little", I said.

"He looks familiar to you. Are you trying to fool us?" he asked.

"Sir, I have said you before that there are only two suits. One is with me and the other is with him. Now, don't blame me for it", I replied with aggression.

"How can you say that he is the one who robbed it?" he questioned.

"Check the footage at the entrance about who left the bank before the robbery. You will find the answer", I replied.

He started to check whether that guy left the bank or not. Now, the footage seemed empty with everyone left out. Suddenly, the video stopped. It means he broke it.

"We did not find him. But, what if he is not that person? We need some more time to investigate on this", the chief of police said.

"You still don't believe me. It's ok. Sometimes even truth doesn't work", I said.

"Sir, we feel him familiar to you. You need to stay in our custody until we find him. Do you know anything of his where about?" he enquired.

"I just know his address. But, I did not find him there", I said and gave the address.

"Don't worry. We will find him as soon as possible. Thanks for the information. Our cops will take care of you", he said and left the place.

"Come with me", a man with about six feet height and muscled body said.

"I wore mask and walked along with him. He sent me into a room and locked it. At least, I can have a piece of mind here. I felt and started observing the room.

It had a small table fan with only one small light at the corner of that room and a chair. I sat on it and sharpened my brain for my next moves.

CHAPTER-22

BIG MISTAKE
FROM BURGLAR

Two days passed, the cops just gave me food and didn't even try to speak with me. But, they have been watching me through the camera. I was feeling lonely out there.

"Is anybody there in this whole world who would like to speak with me?" I shouted.

I screamed it 3 to 4 times for every half an hour. There was no response. This time I started hitting the door. The door sounded really good enough to reach their ears. I used all my energy to break it, but I couldn't make it. I am out of strength now.

"Can anyone for god's sake please open the door?" I shouted again.

Slowly, my voice lowered and my eyes began to close.

"Can….. Anyone….. Please….." I said and became unconscious.

After sometime, someone knocked the door from outside and gave me food in a tray through a hole in the door, which is locked from outside. I ate it with such a speed as if I hadn't seen the food for years.

It's like a hell for me. Finally, I got an idea. I stood up and caught my neck with my both hands and sounded as if the food got struck in my neck. I started acting like I'm in an unconscious stage. This time it worked.

Suddenly, a doctor came running towards me with a full battalion of cops behind him.

He started to push on my chest with both hands. I remained in my position. The force which he used began to rise. If I wait for another second, then surely he will be killing me. So, I suddenly moved up with a deep breath.

All started clapping and praising him.

I just thought "what are these guys up to?" Instead, they should be praising me for such a good action.

I called one of those cops and said, "I want to go home".

He started staring at me. I said it again. They all left the room and locked it.

My drama was all in vain there. Nothing could be done now except waiting for the chief to solve the case. So, I sat idle after such a drama.

"Adam! Wake up", a voice came. I slowly opened my eyes. Someone was standing in front of me. I rubbed my eyes and there you go that was the chief of police.

"Sir", I said.

"I need to talk to you", he said.

"Yeah, sure sir. Go on", I said.

"He started it again. We couldn't catch him even this time. I don't know what to do?" he said with a saddest tone.

"Oh, my god! This is a hard thing to digest sir. So, you finally came to know that I was not the one responsible for all this stuff", I said.

"Sadly, yes. Hope my fellow cops had taken a good care of you", he said sarcastically.

"Yes! Yes! They took care of me like a limited edition guest. I had a great time with them", I said.

"So, would you like to stay some more days here?" he asked.

"No way. I am overwhelmed by your service and it's enough for me. I will leave this place immediately with your permission", I said.

He laughed and said, "OK. You are free now and your taxi is right in front of the building".

"Thank you, sir. For such a wonderful service and I am leaving now", I said and started walking.

"Wait!!" a voice came.

He started walking towards me and said, "Incase if you find any further information please contact us. This case has to be solved as soon as possible. As a citizen it's your duty".

"Sure, sir. How many banks did he rob?" I asked.

"24", he said.

"Ok, sir. I will payback him for all this. Surely, I'll be helping you to solve it. See you again", I said and left the place.

Thank god!! It's a big relief for me now the cops won't be calling me back if he leaves any clues about me. I need a wholesome rest now. So, I drove straight to my home.

CHAPTER-23

PLAN WITH COPS

"What's next?" is the big question which was running in my mind. Now I am a little safer than before, because he came up with two things to me.

One is that he will be robbing and cops will be thinking that it was me. The other is that he wants to kill me. It's never easy with those burglars with superhuman abilities. It would be better I meet him first, before he meets me.

How many banks did he rob? Chief said that the count was 24. So, which bank did he left out? What if we keep an eye on remaining?

It could be better if I meet the cops and help them with their plan. I had no time to think whether to do it or not. He is eagerly waiting to kill me. I don't even want to give him a chance. So, I drove back again to the hell (FBI office).

The office looked really crowded with cops. I think so they might have concluded something about the matter. One of them recognized me and took straight to chief's cabin. He was sitting in his chair thinking madly about the situation.

"Good morning, sir", I said.

"Good morning. What do you want?" he asked me.

"What's happening here?" I asked him in return.

"You asked me about the no of banks he robbed, right? I came to know that there was still only one bank remaining for him to rob", he replied.

"What!!! He robbed all the remaining banks", I said.

"Yes. Sadly, we are trying to protect it. But, somewhere it is running in my mind that we are going to lose him even this time too", chief said.

"Sir, the problem is you are not able to trace him. Because, he is entering the bank strangely and leaving it strangely", I said.

"So, what do you want me to do? We are checking each and every one out there. But, it didn't work", he said.

"We need to let him rob this bank sir", I said.

"Are you mad? You need me to watch it while he is robbing", chief spoke aggressively.

"Let me finish it, sir. We will reply him with the same thing he tried on us. First thing is that you need to reduce the security at the bank. He might not rob it this time if the risk is high", I explained.

"This is like letting a rat to take cheese from the trap easily. I don't know what you are up to?" chief asked without trusting my plan.

"Sir, how can he take the cheese out of it, if the cheese is me", I said which made him think for a while.

"So, you need me to clear the money there and you are the one going to be in there", he said.

"Exactly, sir. Provide me with a Bluetooth and a double barrel gun. I will finish that rat without even touching the cheese", I said.

Chief began to laugh and said, "Pretty cool idea, Mr. Adam. Buckle yourself, I will provide you everything you want. We are not going to miss him this time".

"Sure, sir. This will be a Do or Die thing for me. I won't let him go so easily with that huge money which he robbed. But, there is a thing sir. What if he stops robbing the bank?" I asked him.

"Don't even think of it. He should do it at any cost as we need to catch him. Get ready, Adam. We will be sending you into the locker this evening. I will clear the path for you to get in", chief said.

"Ok, sir. I'm ready. Let's move on", I said.

CHAPTER-24

PAYBACK TIME

I equipped myself with two handguns, a double barrel gun and extra ammo. And I also have a deadly weapon which is my suit. They sent me into the locker providing me with a mike and receiver.

The whole locker was empty. They shifted the entire money to the other place and left me inside. I removed my gloves and touched the walls of the locker to feel its color and acquire it. This makes the others to distract from me.

"Hold your position and wait for my go, Adam", the guy on the mike said.

"Affirmative", I said.

I had nothing to do out there except waiting for that scoundrel to approach me.

"How is everything out there?" I asked the cops.

"Everything's calm and going good", I got a reply.

"No. No. the security camera at the entrance has been broken. He entered in. Hold your positions", I received.

"Don't produce any sign of moments. He will be alerted by it", I said.

"One more camera down, this time it's near the waiting hall. With your order's sir, we would like to start firing", one of those cops said.

"No stay right in your positions. Let him move", chief said.

"There is no sign of him from the cameras. We are not able to see him", one of them said.

"It is because he is changing his color according to the situation", I responded.

"He broke another one. This time it is in the way towards the locker. Adam, can you hear me?" chief asked.

"Yes", I said.

"Stay alert. This is the time we are waiting for. He is yours now. We are not going to let him get away this time. Keep your eyes open", chief said.

"Yes, sir. I am ready to break his neck", I said.

I can hear the foot-steps of that burglar near the locker. But, I don't know how he obtained its keys. He started to open it.

Finally, the locker is opened and four other guys entered it first.

They were shocked by looking at the figure of empty locker. The big boss entered now. He looked similar to me with that suit. I remained quiet in my position and suddenly, I shot two of them right in their heads. They were surprised by that move as they couldn't see me just like their boss. I finished the other two, similarly.

"Ok. I know you are out there. Now, please come to meet me my dear Adam", burglar said.

He found me and I just started walking towards him.

"There you are my boy. Your master plan seemed really brilliant. Fair enough, to catch a thief like me. But, what will you get in return? A small amount of money? An appreciation certificate? Where will you keep it? Join your hands with me my fellow. We will rule everything", he said.

"That was indeed a good speech. But, it doesn't work on my brain. Try something which can make you stay alive from me?" I said with a grunt.

"You are a fool, Adam. Robert gave you such a beautiful life to live and he had shown you a way to earn. You are wasting your energy by stopping me", he said.

"There's no time for words now. Let's finish this thing", I said and gave a blow on his face. He started to bleed from his mouth.

"Yes, let's finish it", he said and kicked me on my knee and grabbed my neck.

I started punching him in his stomach. The grab was getting even tighter. I pulled his hands right now of my neck and punched below his chin. He flew in the air and landed at a distance. I ran towards him and kicked in his stomach. That was a little harder one to bear. It's time to see the man behind the mask.

I pulled out the face mask to see him. You won't believe it. The man I saw was "William". I just ran back and my mind became blank. I was speechless for a moment. I sat in front of him.

"Why? Why William? You had a good Taxi stand, nice employees. What more do you want? You bastard", I screamed and punched him on both the sides of his face.

"Please, let me go Adam. I will tell you everything", William said.

"Do you have a choice?" I asked.

"Actually, the doctor consulted me first for this transplantation. I agreed for it. He said that I need to rob the banks he is going to give me 50% share in it if I help him".

"But, I asked him what if I get caught?"

"So, he said that he needs one more guy to transplant to make the cops turn around him".

"The very next day he met you and said me about you. I said him to proceed and you seemed little brilliant to get even a suit for you. So, I stole it. This is the thing happened out there", William said.

"Why did you kill the doctor?" I asked.

"I killed him so that I can get the total money instead of sharing it", he replied.

"You cunning scoundrel. It's show time now. Get ready to die", I said.

"No, please, let me go I will stop all this things and return all the money", he said.

"I know how to recover the money. Now say good bye to this world", I said and shot him right in his head with my gun. Finally, the burglar is killed.

I removed my mike and started walking towards the entrance. All the cops were waiting for me. They started applauding me for such a good deed and I simply walked from there without even looking at them as I was not one of them. I took my taxi and drove straight away to the seaside.

CHAPTER-25

HAPPY ENDINGS

I sat at the same place where Lisa sat on that day when she thought it was me who robbed the banks.

I removed my gloves and gave a look at my skin. That was a horrible feeling to digest. I raised my head and started watching the calm sea.

It was a beautiful sunset and everything was pleasant there. A man sat beside me. I gave a look at him. He was the chief of police.

"Is everything all right Adam?" he enquired me.

I gave a smile and said "Yes, I think so. Your case has been solved and you can find the money in his taxi stand. I had done my duty as a citizen".

"You really had done your job greatly. We could have never caught him without your help", chief said "So, what's next Mr. Adam? The boss who gave you the job is dead now and how will you be finding another job with a suit on you? Let me help you regain your skin".

I remained silent for a while.

"Speak out, Adam. I will transform you again", chief said.

"It's ok, sir. I am happy with it and I don't even want to try that thing again. What if it shows another effect on me? I cannot risk it again. Thank you, for your suggestion", I replied.

"Ok. What are you going to do now?" he asked me.

"I just thought of meeting Lisa now to say her a heart full thanks", I replied.

"Ok. Then what?" he asked.

"A man said to me to start my carrier as an entrepreneur. I will think of it", I said.

"Ok gentleman, move on. This is my card and you can contact me whenever you want. I'll be there to help you. Bye, for now", he said and left the place.

So, what's next?

Lisa, here I come.

THE END